For my brother Jim, whose imagination has always inspired me,
with love, L.R.

Santa's New Suit
Copyright © 2000 by Laura Rader
Printed in the United States of America. For information address HarperCollins Children's Books,
a division of HarperCollins Publishers, 1350 Avenue of the Americas, New York, NY 10019.
Library of Congress Catalog Card Number: 00-100306
ISBN 0-06-028439-0 — ISBN 0-06-029284-9 (lib. bdg.) — ISBN 0-06-443580-6 (pbk.)
www.harperchildrens.com
Typography by Robbin Gourley

Santa's New Suit
Laura Rader

CLAUS

HarperCollins*Publishers*

It was the week before Christmas.
Santa looked in his closet.
All he could see was red.
Lots of red suits.

He tried one suit on.

It had a tear in it.

He tried on another.

It was too small.

A third was covered in soot stains.

His hats didn't look so good either.

Mrs. Claus was in the living room.
"I need a change," said Santa.
"Tomorrow I'm going to buy a new suit."

"Oh my," said Mrs. Claus.

The next day Santa strolled into town
to buy his new suit.
Everyone knew him.
Everyone was happy to see him.

First Santa went into Nip and Tux.

Then to New Wave.

Beddy Bye was the next stop.

Costumania had more suits than Santa had ever seen.

Then Santa saw THE suit.

Santa tried on the outfit.
It was just what he wanted.

"It has a cap to match,"
said the salesman.
"I'll take it!" said Santa.

Santa wore his new suit home.

"How do you like my new suit?"
he asked.
"Oh my!" said Mrs. Claus.
"I knew you'd like it," said Santa.

Santa went out to show the elves.
"What do you think, fellas?" he said.

The comments were not flattering.

The reindeer did not have a lot of nice things to say either.

The next morning Santa went to Glutz's department store to hear what the children wanted for Christmas.

His visit did not go well.

When Santa got home, he sank into his favorite chair.
"No one likes my new suit," said Santa sadly.
"Not even a little."

Mrs. Claus brought Santa some milk and cookies.
She did not say anything.
She gave him a photo album.

Santa and Mrs. Claus looked at the photographs.
So many happy memories. So many happy faces.
In every picture, Santa was wearing his red suit.

Baby Santa

Young Santa

and Friends

Santa closed the album.
He smiled at Mrs. Claus.
"I have to tell the elves and reindeer something," he said.

"I'm going to wear my red suit on Christmas Eve," he told the elves. "I'm going to wear my red suit on Christmas Eve," he told the reindeer.

Yahoo!

When Christmas Eve came, Santa looked in his closet.
There was a brand-new suit.
And a brand-new cap to match.

It was clean.

It had no holes.

It was just the right size.

It was red.

It was Santa's new suit, and Santa loved it!